DECONSTRUCTED DIETS

PULL APART A PIZZA

by Shalini Vallepur

Minneapolis, Minnesota

© 2021 Booklife Publishing

This edition is published by arrangement with Booklife Publishing.

North American adaptations © 2021 Bearport Publishing Company. All rights reserved. No part of this publication may be reproduced in whole or in part, stored in any retrieval system, or transmitted in any form or by any means, electronic, mechanical, photocopying, recording, or otherwise, without written permission from the publisher.

For more information, write to Bearport Publishing, 5357 Penn Avenue South, Minneapolis, MN 55419. Printed in the United States of America.

Library of Congress Cataloging-in-Publication Data is available at www.loc.gov or upon request from the publisher.

ISBN: 978-1-64747-524-6 (hardcover)
ISBN: 978-1-64747-531-4 (paperback)
ISBN: 978-1-64747-538-3 (ebook)

PHOTO CREDITS

All images are courtesy of Shutterstock.com, unless otherwise specified. With thanks to Getty Images, Thinkstock Photo, and iStockphoto. Front Cover - VWORLD, Morphart Creation, PILart. Recurring Images - VWORLD, mything, AKaiser, PILart, Morphart Creation. 4-5 - Spreadthesign, Bartosz Luczak, mything, Sunnydream, wavebreakmedia, Ansty. 6-7 - dikobraziy, Frame Art, V. Matthiesen, www.petrovvladimir.ru, Carolus. 8-9 - David Franklin, FotoSajewicz, Gts, svariophoto. 10-11 - Alfmaler, Ilike, JLwarehouse, mything, SThom. 12-13 - abogdanska, Brent Hofacker, LightField Studios, Magicleaf, Risha.Bee, Vasilyeva Larisa, PILart, Ansty. 14-15 - Ba_peuceta, Brent Hofacker, etorres, HandmadePictures, lukpedclub, Vector_dream_team, robuart. 16-17 - danm12, Hong Vo, Maquiladora, schwarzhana, yamix, vandycan. 18-19 - El Nariz, Gita Kulinitch Studio, Maks Narodenko, Olga Danylenko, Pektoral, Scisetti Alfio, Tim UR. 20-21 - ducu59us, Martin Kovacik, Ruslan Mitin, zarzamora. 22-23 - Alland Dharmawan, Brent Hofacker, CloudyStock, dikobraziy, Elena Hramova, Sunnydream, Dreamearth, Ricky Edward.

CONTENTS

What Is a Diet? 4

Pizza Perfect 6

Pull Apart a Pizza................... 8

Pizza Crust 10

Sauce 12

Cheese 14

Meat 16

Fruits and Vegetables 18

Smart Swaps................... 20

Pizza around the World 22

Glossary 24

Index 24

WHAT IS A DIET?

A person's diet is made up of the food they eat. The food we eat helps us to grow and be healthy.

Our meals are made from different **ingredients**. It can be difficult to know exactly what is in our food and where it comes from.

Curry is made from lots of different ingredients.

Let's look at all the ingredients in a pizza!

PIZZA PERFECT

Pizza as we know it today comes from Italy.

Margherita pizza

QUEEN MARGHERITA

Margherita pizza was first made in 1889. It was named after Queen Margherita.

When people from Italy moved to the United States, they started opening pizza shops. Over time, pizza began to change.

Pizza comes from Italy, but there are many types from around the world.

PULL APART A PIZZA

Pizza can have few or many **toppings**.

Olive

Almost any vegetable can be put on a pizza.

Ham

Cheese

Mushroom

Pepper

Most pizzas have cheese.

Tomato sauce

Tomato

Pizza crust

Onion

Dessert pizza can have sweet toppings, such as chocolate.

DID YOU KNOW?

Three billion pizzas are sold in the U.S. every year.

Let's learn about each ingredient.

PIZZA CRUST

Every pizza needs a crust! White flour is mixed with other ingredients to make dough.

Wheat · White flour · Dough · Pizza crust

Dough is rolled or stretched into a circle.

Wheat can be made into different kinds of flour. Wheat flour is healthier for you than white flour.

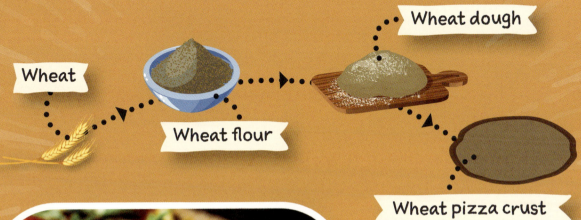

Wheat
Wheat flour
Wheat dough
Wheat pizza crust

Wheat pizza crusts have more **fiber**.

SAUCE

Tomato sauce is usually put on the pizza crust.

Tomatoes are mixed with other ingredients to make sauce.

White sauce

Sweet red sauce

White sauce or sweet red sauces can also be used instead of tomato sauce.

Tomatoes are good for you. However, some tomato sauces have lots of added salt and sugar.

Try making your own healthy sauce.

CHEESE

Most pizzas have cheese. Mozzarella is a good cheese for pizza because it melts easily.

Mozzarella is made from cow or buffalo milk.

Cheddar cheese can also be used on pizzas.

Mozzarella and other cheeses are full of **calcium**. Calcium makes our bones and teeth strong.

Buffalo milk is often used to make fresh mozzarella in Italy.

Mozzarella

Broccoli

Kale

Broccoli and kale also have lots of calcium.

MEAT

Meat, such as ham, is a popular topping on pizzas. Ham is a type of pork. Pork comes from pigs.

Pork is cooked and **sliced** to make ham.

Have you had a ham pizza?

Ham and pepperoni are popular pizza toppings. However, they can be bad for us because they have lots of fat and salt added to them.

Pizza meats

Pepperoni

Try having vegetables on your pizza, too.

FRUITS AND VEGETABLES

Fruits and vegetables are popular pizza toppings.

Tomato

Sliced tomatoes

Olives
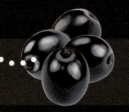

Sliced olives

Tomatoes and olives are fruits.

You can also put pineapple on pizza.

Many kinds of vegetables can be used as pizza toppings!

SMART SWAPS

Pizza is tasty, but it can be unhealthy. Try swapping meat toppings with fruits and veggies.

Vegetable pizza

Pizzas without meat can be eaten by **vegetarians**.

Pizza can be made to fit different diets by changing the ingredients and toppings.

Vegan cheese and fruit and veggie toppings make a pizza vegan.

Vegan pizza

This pizza crust is made of cauliflower. It can be eaten by people who can't eat **gluten**.

Gluten-free pizza

PIZZA AROUND THE WORLD

Pizza is enjoyed all around the world. There are many ways to make pizza.

Deep dish pizza comes from Chicago.

Deep dish pizza

22

Pizza might be topped with curry in parts of India.

Dessert pizzas can be topped with fruit and chocolate. Yum!

Dessert pizza

GLOSSARY

calcium — something found in some food that is good for bones and teeth

fiber — a part of some foods that takes longer for the human body to break down

gluten — a part of wheat that makes dough sticky

ingredients — the different things that are used to make something

sauce — a liquid topping for food

sliced — cut into thin strips

toppings — things that go on something

vegan — foods from a diet in which people do not eat anything that comes from animals, such as meat, cheese, or eggs

vegetarians — people who do not eat meat

INDEX

buffalo 14–15
chocolate 9, 23
crust 9–12, 21
fat 15, 17, 20

fruit 13, 18, 20–21, 23
Italy 6–7, 15
meat 8, 16–17, 20

mozzarella 14–15
pigs 16
vegetables 8, 17–21